Let's Get a Christmas Tree!

By Lori Haskins Houran

Illustrated by Nila Aye

g A GOLDEN BOOK · NEW YORK

Text copyright © 2022 by Lori Haskins Houran
Cover art and interior illustrations copyright © 2022 by Nila Aye
All rights reserved. Published in the United States by Golden Books, an imprint of
Random House Children's Books, a division of Penguin Random House LLC, 1745
Broadway, New York, NY 10019. Golden Books, A Golden Book, A Little Golden Book,
the G colophon, and the distinctive gold spine are registered trademarks of Penguin
Random House LLC.
rhcbooks.com
Educators and librarians, for a variety of teaching tools, visit us at
RHTeachersLibrarians.com
Library of Congress Control Number: 2021947489
ISBN 978-0-593-30653-6 (trade) — ISBN 978-0-593-30654-3 (ebook)
Printed in the United States of America
10 9 8 7 6 5 4 3 2 1

"I'm ready to go!" I said.

I had on my puffiest coat, my fuzziest mittens, and my tallest boots.

Woof! Bo was ready, too!

Dad smiled. "Let's get a Christmas tree!"

At the Christmas tree farm, the snow crunched under our feet.

"Our perfect tree is here," Mom said. "I just know it."

We walked up and down the rows of pretty
green trees. Bo sniffed while we searched.
Crunch, crunch, crunch.
Sniff, sniff, sniff.

"How about this one?" asked Dad.
"Hmm. It's a little flat on the side," Mom said.

"How about this one?" asked Mom.
"Maybe," said Dad. "It's just a teensy bit crooked."

"Definitely *not* this one," I said.
It was taller than our house!

Woof! barked Bo.

He was sniffing a tree. A *perfect* tree! It wasn't
too flat or too crooked or too tall. It was just right.

"Look!" I cried.
"How lovely!" said Mom.
Dad patted Bo's head. "Good boy."

A helper wrapped up the tree and tied it on top
of our car.

"Thank you," Mom called. "Merry Christmas!"

On our way home, it got dark. The houses on the street glowed with Christmas lights.

"WOW!" I said.
We slowed down at a big house.
It was lit up from top to bottom!

There was a giant nutcracker by the door,
and a sleigh on the roof—with Santa and his
reindeer!

Our own house didn't have *quite* as many
decorations, but it was just as beautiful.
"I'll carry the tree inside," said Dad.
"I'll help!" I said.

We had cocoa and cookies to warm up.

Then Dad turned on some Christmas music, and Mom took out the ornaments.

"Here you go." She gave me a sparkly green ball with my baby picture on it.

"I was so little!"

"Yes, you were." Mom gave me a tight squeeze.

Dad put a wooden snowman on the tree.
Mom added a candy cane made of yarn.

"Don't forget Bo's." Dad passed me an ornament shaped like a bone. I hung it down low, where Bo could see it.

We kept going until every branch was full.

Dad lifted me to his shoulders.
"Time for the star," he said.

I slipped our shiny gold star onto the very top of the tree.

"Now I wish it was Christmas morning!" I said.
Woof! agreed Bo.

And pretty soon . . .

. . . it was!

MERRY CHRISTMAS!